Barbie

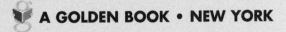

Barbie Loves Weddings

By Mary Man-Kong
Cover photography by Joe Dias, Shirley Ushirogata, Bill Couuts,
Greg Roccia, Lisa Collins, and Judy Tsuno
Interior photography by Mark Adams, Shirley Ushirogata, Cheryl Fetrick,
Greg Roccia, Lawrence Cassel, Scott Meskill, and Judy Tsuno

A GOLDEN BOOK • NEW YORK

BARBIE and associated trademarks and trade dress are owned by, and used under license from, Mattel, Inc.
© 2004 Mattel, Inc. All Rights Reserved.
Published in the United States by Golden Books, an imprint of Random House Children's Books, a division of
Random House, Inc., New York, and simultaneously in Canada by Random House of Canada Limited, Toronto.
No part of this book may be reproduced or copied in any form without written permission from the copyright owner.
Golden Books, A Golden Book, and the G colophon are registered trademarks of Random House, Inc.
Library of Congress Control Number: 2003105377   ISBN: 0-375-82742-0
www.goldenbooks.com   Printed in the United States of America   10 9 8 7 6 5 4 3 2

Barbie loves weddings—and she's especially excited about the wedding of two of her best friends, Stephanie and Eric!

Stephanie asks Barbie to be her maid of honor. Barbie can't wait to help out.

"I know the perfect place for you to get married," Barbie says.

Stephanie and Eric's first date was at the beach, so Barbie takes them to the Ocean Club.

"You can have the ceremony on the beach," Barbie says. "Then the reception can be in the club."

"What a great idea," says Stephanie.

The next day, Barbie and Stephanie go to the florist to pick out the flowers. Stephanie's favorite flowers are roses, lilies, and tulips.

Stephanie decides to have white lilies in her bouquet and have the bridesmaids carry purple tulips and roses.

Next, Barbie and Stephanie go to pick out their dresses. Kira, another bridesmaid, joins them. Stephanie finds the perfect wedding gown, and she chooses a pretty pink dress for the bridesmaids and flower girl.

"It's beautiful," Barbie says. "Pink is my favorite color."

Barbie pulls Kira aside to discuss the wedding present. "Since Stephanie and Eric are going to Hawaii for their honeymoon, how about getting them snorkeling gear?" Barbie whispers.

"Cool idea," says Kira. "Let's go to the sporting goods store tomorrow."

Two weeks before the wedding, Barbie throws
Stephanie a bridal shower.
"Surprise!" everyone shouts.

Stephanie loves the surprise bridal shower.
She especially loves the snorkeling gear that
Barbie and Kira give her.

"Thanks, guys," says Stephanie.

The big day is finally here! Stephanie looks beautiful in her white wedding gown, and Eric looks very handsome in his tuxedo.

"Smile!" says the photographer as she takes their picture.

"It was so much fun helping my friends and sharing in their special day," Barbie says. "That's why I love weddings!"